Luke Lively
and
The Castle of Sleep

Debbie White

Illustrated by Judy Brown

OXFORD
UNIVERSITY PRESS

OXFORD
UNIVERSITY PRESS

Great Clarendon Street, Oxford OX2 6DP

Oxford University Press is a department of the University of Oxford.
It furthers the University's objective of excellence in research, scholarship,
and education by publishing worldwide in

Oxford   New York

Auckland   Cape Town   Dar es Salaam   Hong Kong   Karachi
Kuala Lumpur   Madrid   Melbourne   Mexico City   Nairobi
New Delhi   Shanghai   Taipei   Toronto

With offices in

Argentina   Austria   Brazil   Chile   Czech Republic   France   Greece
Guatemala   Hungary   Italy   Japan   Poland   Portugal   Singapore
South Korea   Switzerland   Thailand   Turkey   Ukraine   Vietnam

Oxford is a registered trade mark of Oxford University Press
in the UK and in certain other countries

Text © Debbie White 2000

First published 2000
This edition 2005

British Library Cataloguing in Publication Data
Data available

ISBN: 978-0-19-918438-5

5 7 9 10 8 6

Available in packs
Stage 15 More Stories A Pack of 6:
ISBN: 978-0-19-918436-1
Stage 15 More Stories A Class Pack:
ISBN: 978-0-19-918443-9
Guided Reading Cards also available:
ISBN: 978-0-19-918445-3

Cover artwork by Mike Spoor

Printed in Great Britain by
Ashford Colour Press, Gosport, Hants.

1

The next best thing

It is just after lunch at the Ministry for
Fairytale Regeneration (M.F.R. for short) and
the Chief Computer Officer, Ron Smallweed,
is about to make a horrible discovery.

He has asked Fickle Finger, the M.F.R.'s
awesomely powerful computer, to access the
Sleeping Beauty File and before he can say
'Witches' Knickers' it's on screen. All the
Sleeping Beauties that have ever been scroll
past, neatly listed in date order. And the last
one on the list is Aurora Rose Rams-Botham,
born Cutforth Castle, June 1885 into a family
with royal connections, but absolutely no
cash.

At the moment, she is still snoring away
happily in a forgotten room, in the tallest
turret of Cutforth Castle. She is due to be

woken up tomorrow by dark and handsome Prince Hugo. But Hugo has other ideas. He's already madly in love with his Personal Fitness Trainer, Paula. He plans to live happily ever after with her instead.

In fact, they're just about to run off together.

'They can't,' shouts Jackson Bigwood, Minister in Charge at the M.F.R.

'That's not allowed. Are you sure Fickle Finger has got it right?'

'Fickle doesn't make mistakes,' says Ron, looking hurt.

'In that case,' says the Minister, 'we'll have to find someone else. And fast. Ask Fickle for a list of other suitable princes.'

Quick as a flash, Ron keys in the request. Seconds later, he's tearing off the list from the printer. He looks at it. Then he turns it over.

'There's nothing on it,' he wails. 'It's completely blank.'

'Give it here,' says the Minister crossly. 'Let me have a look.'

But even with his reading glasses on, he can see that Ron's right.

'What does it mean?' asks Ron.

'It means,' says the Minister, 'that we've run out of princes.'

'What are we going to do?'

'Ask Fickle for a list of the NEXT BEST THING.'

Ron looks blank.

'Look,' says the Minister slowly. 'Supposing Prince Hugo's great grandfather –'

'King Havelock,' interrupts Ron.

'– Hadn't married Prince Hugo's great grandmother, Queen Hilda.'

'But he did,' says Ron. 'He was famous for it. People said it was the fairytale wedding of the century.'

'Yes I know that,' says the Minister, who's starting to sound cross. 'But supposing he hadn't. What if he'd never married at all? Who would have been next in line for the throne, then?'

'Um,' says Ron, hazarding a guess. 'One of King Havelock's nephews or nieces?'

'He didn't have any. He was an only child.'

'In that case,' says Ron, 'we'd better ask Fickle.'

They turn to look at the screen. Fickle, using his awesomely powerful artificial intelligence, has already come up with an answer.

'Luke Lively?' says the Minister. 'What sort of stupid name is that? And who is he? Where does he live? What does he look like? Where does he go to school?'

'Hold on,' says Ron, his fingers flying over the keyboard. 'I can't type that fast.'

'Oh my word!' gasps the Minister as the answers pop onto Fickle's screen. 'There must be some mistake.'

Ron's about to say, 'Fickle doesn't . . .' But the words stick in his throat.

Fickle has down-loaded Luke's school photo, which is very unfair. With his hair gelled and parted in the middle, his spotty  chin and immaculately pressed shirt and smart tie, he looks like an alien from another planet. (Even his mum wouldn't recognize him.)

He reads the list of Luke's interests:

Football
Computer Games
Girls . . .

He reads the list of Luke's pet hates:

School
Having a shower
Girls . . .

He stares at a gruesomely detailed picture of Luke's bedroom: 23, Willow Drive, Osgathorpe.

He can even see the week-old peanut butter sandwich festering under Luke's bed. He thinks of Aurora Rose Rams-Botham fast

asleep in Cutforth Castle.
Aurora Rose, who listed her
interests as:

Croquet
Sketching
Playing the piano
Taking anything mechanical apart . . .

And her pet hates as:

Spiders
Rice pudding
Miss Wibberley (her governess)
Not being allowed to take things apart.

Somehow he just can't see it working.

'It was always going to be a tricky one.
Even with Prince Hugo,' the Minister is
saying. 'After all, things have moved on a bit
in the last hundred years. Think about all the
things we have now that they didn't have
then:

'Space Travel.'

'Motorways.'

'Supermarkets.'

'Computers.'

'Votes for Women.'

'Take away pizzas. Oven chips. Soft toilet paper,' says Ron.

'They are both going to have to make adjustments,' continues the Minister. 'It's going to be a rough ride. Still. We haven't got much choice. If our Sleeping Beauty isn't woken up, the whole cycle's down the pan. Kaput! No more Sleeping Beauties ever. Then before you can say Rumplestiltskin, the whole Ministry's being downsized and we're out on our ears.'

'Eeek!' squeaks Ron.

'Exactly,' says the Minister. 'So we can't afford to make any mistakes. We need help.'

'Anyone in mind?' asks Ron.

'The best F.G. in the business,' says the Minister.

'And who's that?' says Ron, desperately trying to think of all the Fairy Godmothers he's ever met.

'Don't you know?' snaps the Minister.

'Is it that short fat one? You know, the one we had to use when we had trouble with Cinderella?'

'No! Don't be silly. It's Gretl Greta of course.'

'Gretl Greta!' gasps Ron. Of course he has heard of her.

'Only problem is, she's on a climbing holiday in the Swiss Alps. But a quick message on her pager and she'll be back here in no time at all.'

'Wizard!' says Ron.

2

Castle ahoy

By the time Gretl arrived at the Ministry she was in a very bad mood.

'Right, Bigwood,' she growled. 'You've just called me back from the first decent holiday I've had in two hundred years. You'd better have a good explanation.'

She banged her walking boots down on the Minister's desk. As the Minister began to fill Gretl in on all the details, she stopped looking quite so cross and started to look interested.

'Mmn,' she said. 'How extraordinary! What did you say this young man's name was, again? And he's had no experience of being a prince at all?'

'None whatsoever,' said the Minister. 'So you can see why we had to call you in.'

'Of course,' said Gretl. 'You did the right thing. Don't worry, Bigwood, Gretl Greta's on the case.'

Luke Lively, hanging around the kitchen of 23, Willow Drive, didn't know that Gretl was about to change his life for ever, so he was whining about being bored. It was a tactic he often used on his mum and it always got excellent results.

'There's nothing to do. I wish something exciting would happen. It's Saturday and you're going to spend all day working. You won't pay me any attention at all.'

'You're right. Nothing exciting is going to happen,' said Luke's mum. 'Not until I've finished balancing Mr Boggit's books anyway.' (Mrs Lively was a Chartered Accountant.) 'So you can nip down to the shops for me. I've run out of milk.'

Luke said nothing.

'Here's some money,' said his mum. She knew she was going to be working all day and she felt guilty about it. 'You can spend the change on sweets.'

'Thanks, Mum!' said Luke, giving her a

quick hug before rushing out of the back
door. 'And when I come back, I'll be really
cheerful. Promise!'

He leapt into the saddle of his mountain
bike and sped off in the direction of the
shops. He'd just made up his mind to buy a
bag of super-sour cherries when he realized
he was going the wrong way. He was
riding down Willow Drive and
away from the shops.

'Jumping
jellyfish!' he muttered
and tried to brake. But nothing
happened. The bike kept rolling
down the hill. At the bottom, it
turned left and very soon he was
heading out into the countryside.

'Juggling jeroboams,' he shouted as his
bike took a sudden turn off the road and
onto a rutted farm track.

'H-e-e-e-l-p!' he wailed as the bike headed off across country.

Poor Luke. His legs had been whizzing round so fast on the pedals, they felt like jelly. Then just as he was thinking he couldn't take any more, the bike suddenly stopped. He somersaulted over the handlebars and rolled into a muddy puddle at the foot of a large oak tree.

'Hah!' said a voice.

Luke looked around. At first he couldn't see anyone. Then a little old lady appeared from behind the tree. She was wearing a tweed suit and sensible shoes. '*There* you are,' she said. 'Not much to look at are you? Not even a decent horse.'

She poked Luke's bike with her stick.

Poor Luke. Not much to look at! He couldn't help being a bit spotty. Everyone was at his age. Still, that didn't stop him feeling sensitive about it. And how dare she poke his bike like that!

He glared at her, but she took no notice. 'If

you hurry, you'll make it in time. Down the hill and through Dazely Wood – you can't miss it once you hit the old road.'

'Miss what?' asked Luke, bewildered.

'Sleeping Beauty's Castle of course,' she said, starting to turn away.

Luke's mouth dropped open. He looked like a stranded fish gasping for air.

'Wait a minute,' he said. 'Only I thought you said Sleeping Beauty's Castle.'

'I did,' she said.

She's completely bonkers, he thought.

'You haven't got a mobile phone have you?' he asked nervously. 'Then I could ring my mum and ask her to come and fetch me.'

'Good grief,' she snorted. 'Whatever next? Jack getting his mum to help him climb the Beanstalk? I ask you.'

'Ask me what?' said Luke, bewildered. 'And who's Jack?'

She didn't reply. She just strode off. He didn't hear the 'bleep, bleep, bleep' as she rang the M.F.R. number. 'Ron. It's Gretl. He's on track for the castle. Due fourteen hundred hours.'

Luke wasn't at all sure what to do next. He could wait and hope someone normal turned up. Or . . . He sighed and picked up his bike. Sleeping Beauty's Castle. Honestly. Who did she think he was?

Fifteen minutes later, at two o'clock exactly, Luke arrived at the gates of a very large and imposing castle. He could just see its turrets peeking out from a great thicket of roses.

That's funny, he thought. His mum was a keen member of the 'Keep up a Castle Trust', but he didn't remember visiting this one. Never mind, the castle was bound to be on the phone. All he had to do was to knock on the door and ask if he could ring his mum. The only problem was, he could see the castle's massive oak front door, but he couldn't reach it. There were too many thorns.

Then a cheerful thought struck him. If there was a front door, there was bound to be a back door too, wasn't there? Dropping his bike to the ground, he scrambled round to see if he was right.

3

Kiss, kiss

'He's supposed to hack his way through, not go round the back!' said the Minister. He'd been tracking Luke's progress on Fickle's monitor.

'It doesn't matter,' said Ron. 'As long as he gets inside, nips up to the tower and wakes Aurora Rose with a kiss.'

'That's the bit I'm really worried about,' said the Minister. 'I just can't see it happening.'

'Hello? Anyone at home?'

Luke turned the back-door handle carefully. He'd had a pretty weird day so far and he wasn't going to feel safe until he was back home. He stepped inside. So far, so good. And someone was there too. He could see a woman wearing a white mob-cap and a long dress and apron, sitting in a chair by a huge, black cooking range.

Phew! he thought, feeling better. He must be in a living history museum. He'd been to one with the school. Actors dressed up and pretended to be people from history. It was really good.

He tiptoed over and touched the woman gently on the shoulder. She stopped snoring, but she didn't wake up. Even when he shouted really loudly in her ear. She's probably a bit deaf, he thought, trying to stay calm. I'll just have to find someone who isn't.

He found the servants' staircase tucked away in the far corner of the room.

'If I go up here,' he said out loud, trying to sound brave, 'I expect I'll come to the main bit of the castle.' He was right.

At first he thought there was no one about. Then he spotted a parlour maid sprawled out fast asleep on the stairs of the Great Hall. A butler, head tipped back and mouth wide open, was sitting bolt upright on a small hard chair by the great oak front door. He looked very uncomfortable, but he was fast asleep too.

Luke could feel his heart doing a very tricky tap dance inside his chest. Of course he didn't believe in fairy stories. No one his age did. But he was beginning to think that finding a castle, covered in roses and full of sleeping people was too much of a coincidence.

He had this feeling that at the very top of the castle, there was going to be a princess fast asleep and waiting for a handsome prince to wake her up.

If there was, it wouldn't do any harm to take a look, would it? After all, *he* wasn't the handsome prince she'd been waiting for, was he?

'Oh help,' gasped Luke, still a bit out of breath from climbing the two hundred stairs to the top of the castle's tallest turret. He hadn't really expected to find a princess. But there she was.

He stood on a stool at the side of an enormous four poster bed, and looked down into the face of the sleeping Aurora Rose. So this is what Sleeping Beauty looks like, he thought.

To be honest, he was a bit disappointed. He had expected her to look like a fairytale princess. You know, long silky hair, soft downy skin, fragile beauty – that sort of stuff. But she didn't look fragile at all. In fact, she looked rather solid. There was something about the set of her mouth, the jut of her chin and the regal outline of her nose that made him feel rather weedy and pathetic.

He was beginning to feel deflated, like the last balloon left at the end of the party. Suddenly, he remembered what came next in the story.

'Oh yuk!' he said, with a shudder. 'There's no way I'm going to k . . .'

But before he had time to finish the sentence, he felt a bony hand grip him by the back of the neck. It was Gretl.

'Give her a kiss, Luke,' she said with a steely smile. 'If you don't, I'll turn you into a worm.'

'What sort of worm?' said Luke, alarmed. 'And how do you know my name?'

'Never you mind. Just do it.'

So he did, but very, very quickly and with his eyes closed.

'All right,' said Gretl. 'I suppose that will do.'

And luckily, it did.

Aurora Rose opened her eyes for the first time in a hundred years and came face to face with Luke. What a horrible shock! She'd been dreaming about a tall, dark and handsome prince. Instead she saw a very ordinary-looking boy with a dirty face and a shock of wild, curly brown hair, wearing the most peculiar clothes (jeans, trainers, football shirt). She started to scream.

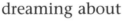

Gretl leaned forward and gave her a poke in the ribs.

'Stop it at once,' she snapped. 'You're awake aren't you? If it wasn't for Luke, you would have slept on for ever. Imagine that.'

Aurora sniffed and looked at Luke sideways from under her eyelashes. He was jiggling around awkwardly. He always did that when he was embarrassed.

'Right,' he said. 'I've kissed her. She's woken up. Now I'm off home.'

'Not unless you take Aurora with you.'

Luke looked at Gretl in disbelief.

'There is no way,' he said firmly, 'I'm taking a GIRL home. What would my mum say?'

'And there is absolutely no way,' said Aurora quickly, 'that I'd go anywhere with *him*. I never go anywhere without Miss Wibberley as chaperone.'

'What's a chaperone?' asked Luke.

'Goodness,' said Aurora. 'Don't you know *that*? She's someone who makes sure you're never, *ever* alone with a young man. Especially if he comes from an unsuitable social background.'

'Unsuitable social background?' repeated Luke. He hadn't a clue what she was talking about.

'You don't need to worry about that any more,' said Gretl. 'Things are much more relaxed these days. Too relaxed if you ask me. And anyway, dear Miss Wibberley ran off just before you pricked your finger. She didn't fancy the hundred year sleep. As for Mama and Papa, they were on six months' holiday in the South of France. They missed everything. Never mind that their only daughter needed them at home. Always were a very selfish couple. Still, no use crying over spilt milk.'

'I don't believe you,' said Aurora, her voice suddenly sounding all trembly. 'You're making it up.'

Luke looked horrified. 'It would be a very horrible thing to have made up,' he said hotly.

Gretl looked at Luke in surprise. Maybe he

wasn't such a selfish little twerp after all.

'You're right,' she said quite gently, 'it would have been. But I'm very much afraid it's the truth.'

At this point, Gretl decided she had to get a grip on herself. The last time she had got emotionally involved in a case, well . . . she shuddered. She only had to catch sight of a piece of gingerbread and she came over all funny.

'Is your mother at home, Luke?' Gretl asked, pulling herself together.

'Yes,' said Luke. 'And she's going to be really worried. I only went out to get some milk and I've been gone for hours.'

'There you are then,' said Gretl to Aurora. 'As you're minus both parents and a governess, Luke's mother can act as a chaperone.'

'I don't think . . .' Luke started to say, but then he stopped.

Most parents would run a mile at the thought of taking in a complete stranger. But Luke's mum wasn't like most parents. The *more* friends he brought home, the happier she was. She said it made the house feel warm and lived-in. So perhaps she wouldn't think twice about taking a poor orphaned friend of his under her wing. Would she?

29

4

The promise

'I've got one of those on my new safety cycle,' said Aurora, looking at Luke's mountain bike which was still lying on the grass outside the castle. She was pointing at the gear lever.

'The Victorians didn't have bikes with gears,' said Luke quickly, hoping she wasn't going to ask him how they worked.

'Of course we did,' she said scathingly. 'They're very useful on hills.' She paused for a second and then she said: 'Is it terribly hilly where your castle is?'

Luke thought about 23, Willow Drive.

'No,' he said. 'And I don't live in a castle. I live in a three bedroomed semi-detached house.'

'Goodness,' said Aurora. 'Only three bedrooms! Where do all your servants sleep?'

Oh dear, thought Luke. He never answered

questions at school if he could help it. Now it looked as if he was going to have to answer lots. He was about to start explaining, when Gretl came out of the castle.

'I've left Cook in charge,' she said. 'I've told her you'll be back as soon as you've sorted out a few things.'

'What sort of things?' asked Aurora suspiciously. Everything had always been sorted out for her.

'The Twenty-First Century,' said Gretl, briskly.

At first, Aurora would not get on the crossbar of Luke's bicycle.

'You'll see my legs,' she said.

Luke couldn't see how. She was wearing a long skirt, striped cotton stockings and little black button up boots.

'I couldn't care less about that,' he said, 'I'm more worried about something getting trapped in the wheels. That's even supposing I can cycle with you on the bike as well.'

'Perhaps we should take the motor car instead?' suggested Aurora.

'Great,' said Luke. 'As long as my bike will fit in the back. What sort of car is it and who's going to drive?'

'It's the very latest Peugeot,' said Aurora. 'And normally Papa does. He used to make Williams, our chauffeur walk in front with the red flag. Poor Williams. Sometimes he had to run because Papa drives terribly fast.'

'Williams must be a very quick runner,' said Luke, looking impressed.

'Oh, he is,' said Aurora, nodding in agreement. 'Papa never drives less than four miles an hour!'

'My mum got booked for speeding once,' said Luke. 'She was doing ninety on the motorway. I told her to slow down, but she wouldn't listen.'

'Don't be silly,' said Aurora crushingly. 'No one could possibly drive that fast. It wouldn't be safe. I suppose you mean nine miles an hour, but I still don't believe you.'

Luke opened his mouth to argue, but what was the point? She'd find out soon enough about cars and motorways and traffic. He almost felt sorry for her. Almost, but not quite. A little bit of him was looking forward to boasting how much better things were these days. (Well, they are, aren't they?)

As it happened, they couldn't use the car. Miss Wibberley and Williams the chauffeur had run away in it. They couldn't use Luke's bike either. With Aurora on board Luke couldn't get it to move.

'It's no good,' he said. 'We won't make it. Anyway, I think you'd better stay here for a bit. At least until I've explained things to my mum. I'll come back tomorrow.'

'Promise!' said Aurora dramatically.
'Because apart from the castle servants and
Gretl, you're the only person I know in the
whole wide world. Everyone else is dead!'

Luke squirmed. He looked shifty. He didn't
want to be the only person she knew in the
whole wide world. It sounded a very
responsible thing to be and so far, the only
thing he'd ever been responsible for was
cleaning out his hamster. (And sometimes he
forgot to do that.)

'Well,' he said, desperately looking for a way out, 'I don't mean to sound horrible or anything, but . . .'

'Promise you'll come back,' said Gretl, 'or I'll turn you into a . . .'

'Worm,' said Luke miserably.

'Exactly,' said Gretl. 'Then I'll chop you in half with a spade.'

'Ooh,' squealed Aurora, 'how horrid.'

'All right, I PROMISE,' said Luke. It didn't look as if he had much choice. Besides, it wasn't every day that you got to meet a real live Victorian and he was also beginning to feel a bit sorry for her. Even if she was irritating and bossy.

'Right,' said Gretl. 'Since Cutforth isn't on the phone, I'll give you the number of my mobile. Now hop it. Out of the castle gates, first left and you'll be home in no time.'

And he was.

5

Home for tea

'What took you so long?' said Luke's mum. 'Hand over the milk. I'm gasping for a cup of tea.'

Oh no, thought Luke, I didn't get any!

'Thanks,' said his mum, picking up a carton from the kitchen table. 'Any change?'

Luke was amazed. Where had that milk come from? It hadn't been there a minute ago. He whirled round, expecting to see Gretl standing close behind him.

'What's the matter?' asked his mum. 'What have you been up to?'

'Nothing,' he said, jiggling around awkwardly.

It was as if Gretl still had a bony grip on his neck.

'Mum, there's something I need to tell you . . .'

Then, (and this was the worst bit,) his mum came and put her arm round him and gave him a big hug. 'You know you can tell me anything, don't you?' she said in a warm, treacly voice.

'I met this girl,' he said, still squirming. 'On my way to the shops.'

'It's all right to talk to girls you know. They don't bite,' said his mum. 'So what's she like? Does she go to your school? Is she pretty?'

'Not specially,' said Luke. 'And she's bossy. She's made me promise I'll see her tomorrow.'

'Are you going to?' asked Mrs Lively, trying not to sound too interested.

'I'll have to,' said Luke. 'Since I said I would.'

'Really?' Mrs Lively was impressed. 'So next time you promise to clean up your room, you'll do it, will you?'

Luke gave his mum a withering look.

'Where does this girl live and does she have a name?'

'Cutforth Castle. And it's Aurora.'

Luke's mum blinked.

'Cutforth CASTLE! Is it somewhere near here? I've never heard of it. Do her parents work there?'

'Er, no. She hasn't got any parents,' said Luke.

'How awful!' said Mrs Lively with feeling. She didn't have a mum or dad either and she missed them dreadfully. 'Does she live with an aunt or something?'

'She's got a sort of godmother,' said Luke, trying to sound as vague as possible. He didn't fancy having to explain about Gretl as well.

'Why don't you give the poor girl a ring and ask her if she'd like to come for tea? We'll have pizza, chips, and chocolate whip.'

Luke dialled Gretl's number.

'Hello,' he said, when she answered. 'I was wondering if Aurora . . .'

'Just a mo',' said Gretl briskly, 'I'll hand you over.'

Aurora took the phone gingerly, as if she thought it was going to explode.

'AURORA ROSE RAMS- BOTHAM SPEAKING.'

'It's me, Luke,' he said, hurriedly holding the phone away from his ear. 'And there's no need to shout. I was just ringing to see if you'd like to come over tomorrow. Mum says she'll pick you up about five o'clock and take you home again later, if that's all right?'

He was desperately hoping it wouldn't be. He knew from doing the Victorians at school that they had all sorts of boring, complicated rules about tea-times and visiting. He was expecting her to say something snooty. But she didn't. In fact she sounded quite excited.

'What will we have for tea, do you think?'

'Pizza and chips,' said Luke.

'Don't forget the chocolate whip,' shouted his mum, who'd been listening in from the kitchen.

'How exotic,' Aurora said. 'And I can't wait to try some carbonated water with colour, sulphite ammonia, caramel, sweetener, phosphoric acid, sodium citrate, preservative and citric acid.'

'What's going on?' said the Minister, looking hard at Fickle's monitor. 'How does she know about cola?'

'Gretl gave her a quick whizz through the

last hundred years on her laptop.'

'Excellent,' said the Minister. 'And what did she make of that?'

'The laptop? Oh, she said she'd read about it in the castle library. She gave quite a good account of Charles Babbage's design for a mechanical, programmable computer.'

You could see Ron was impressed.

'No. Not the laptop,' snarled the Minister. 'I meant the Twenty-First Century. What did she think?'

'She said, "It sounds wonderful, but so does rice pudding until you try it." '

'I like rice pudding,' said the Minister. 'We used to have it with prunes at school.'

'Horrible,' said Ron.

Mrs Lively liked to be on time and they arrived at the castle a bit early.

'My goodness,' she exclaimed as she pulled up outside the gates. 'Does Aurora really live here? I can't believe I haven't heard of the place before.'

'It's never been open to the public,' said Luke quickly.

'I don't expect she'd mind me taking a peek,' said Mrs Lively.

She was just about to get out, when Luke leapt from the car, saying, 'Stay there, Mum. I don't think traipsing round a castle is a good idea. Not when you've had such a tiring day at work.'

Mrs Lively looked surprised. Luke never normally worried about how tired she was. Still, she didn't want to discourage him from being thoughtful, so she said, 'Maybe you're right. I'll just put on a tape while you go and fetch her.'

As his mum leaned back and prepared to sing along to her favourite tracks, Luke shot off to find Aurora.

Mrs Lively was still singing when she spotted Luke coming back along the drive. What she saw made her stop, blink and rub

her eyes. But when she looked again, the
view was still the same.

Luke had a girl with him. A girl wearing a
hat, lace gloves, striped stockings, black
button up boots and carrying a velvet purse
and a parasol. How unusual, thought Mrs
Lively, rather bewildered, but she gave them
a friendly wave.

She was still looking puzzled when Luke and Aurora reached the car.

'I'll sit in front,' said Luke, rushing to open the front passenger door. 'You can get in the back.'

But Aurora wasn't used to being told what to do.

'I always sit next to Papa when he drives. You may sit in the back, Luke,' she said firmly.

Mrs Lively gave her a warm smile as she got in the front passenger seat.

'I'm Luke's mum,' she said. 'You must be Aurora.'

'Aurora Rose Rams-Botham,' said Aurora a little stiffly. 'I am very pleased to meet you.'

'Well, Aurora Rose Rams-Botham, I'm very pleased to meet you too. And that's a really lovely straw hat you're wearing,' said Mrs Lively, leaning over and snapping Aurora's seat belt in place. 'But you'll have to take it off, or you'll block my view.'

Normally, Luke's mum enjoyed speeding

along in the car, but having Aurora in the passenger seat was like driving with a very young and incredibly nosey child. She wanted to touch everything and couldn't sit still for a second.

'Ooh,' she squealed excitedly as she pushed a button and the electric windows flew up and down. 'How do they do that? And what does this do?'

'NO!' screeched Luke's mum as Aurora pulled on the hand brake. There was a strong smell of burning rubber from the tyres. The car slid to a halt.

'Now, Aurora,' said Mrs Lively. 'I want you to sit tight on your hands until we get home. Do you understand?'

Aurora nodded. 'I . . .'

Luke's mum gave her a look.

They drove home in total silence, even when Mrs Lively put her foot down to overtake a lorry and narrowly missed an oncoming car. Luke was impressed. Aurora went a ghastly green colour, but she didn't move a muscle. Then, when they got home, she opened the car door, got out and promptly fainted.

Luke had to help his mum carry her indoors.

'Waft her with the newspaper,' she said. 'I'll try and get her boots off.'

'Good grief!' puffed Mrs Lively. 'No wonder the poor girl passed out. She must be suffocating with all these clothes on. Look, she's wearing a petticoat and frilly drawers. And every last thing has been hand stitched. There's even a monogram embroidered on her purse.'

Mrs Lively picked it up and peered at it closely.

'There are two heraldic-looking rams and some sort of motto. It's written so small I can hardly read it. What does it say: *Fear not the Sheep?* Oh, silly me, it's *Fear not the Sleep*. How odd! Do you know, the last time I saw clothes like these was in a museum. I'd give anything to know where she got them.'

'I don't think,' Luke said carefully, 'that the shop's still in business.'

6

Why can't she go somewhere else?

'More chips?' asked Luke's mum with an approving smile. It was nice to see a girl with such a healthy appetite. So many of them were on diets these days.

'Yes please, Mrs Lively!' said Aurora. 'AND pizza. And cola. And tomato ketchup. Then I should like some chocolate whip with hundreds and thousands and some of that squirty cream out of a tube. If you have some, I should very much like to try crisps. I'm most terribly hungry. It seems like an age since I had anything to eat and you're such a wonderful cook.'

'Hmn,' snorted Luke. His mum a wonderful cook! Still, he couldn't help watching in fascination as Aurora tucked into extra fries with sauce, demolished three bowls of chocolate whip and munched through two packets of crisps.

When it looked as though she'd finally stopped eating, Mrs Lively said, 'Right. I've got some accounts to do. Luke, you can clear the table and I'd like a nice cup of tea please. Strong and not too much milk.'

Luke made a face.

'Don't worry, Mrs Lively,' said Aurora sweetly. 'I shall ring for the maid and organize tea.'

Luke's mum laughed. They could still hear her laughing in the front room.

'Did I say something amusing?' asked Aurora.

'We haven't GOT a maid,' said Luke. 'People don't have them any more. At least, not unless they've got loads of money and we haven't.'

'Oh,' said Aurora. 'So who does all the work then?'

Luke didn't know where to start explaining, so he simply said, 'The dishwasher will do those,' and he pointed at the pile of plates on the kitchen table.

'Dishwasher?' said Aurora. 'I thought you said you didn't have any servants.'

'No! It's that white thing over there.' He nodded carelessly in the direction of the sink. 'You load it up, while I take Mum a cup of tea.'

When he came back, she had just loaded the washing machine with dirty plates, knives and forks.

'Simple!' she said, slamming the door and pressing the extra fast spin button. She turned to Luke with a big smile. 'What happens next?'

As soon as she heard the sound of all her best china being smashed into thousands of tiny pieces, Luke's mum came running. 'What on earth . . . ?'

She leapt forward, turning the machine off
at the wall. Then she bent down and peered
into the drum. She stood up slowly.

'OK,' she said. 'Tell me what's been going on. I want to know why Aurora's dressed up like a Victorian fashion plate, what happened to her parents and why she's just loaded my washing machine full of dishes. And it had better be good.'

'Oh dear,' said the Minister, picking up the phone. 'This is going to be tricky. Gretl!' he said, bellowing into the mouthpiece, 'I want you at Luke's house immediately!'

'Don't worry,' said Ron soothingly. 'Mrs Lively won't believe a word they tell her.'

The Minister looked doubtful, but Ron was right. She didn't.

'I stopped believing in fairy stories years ago,' said Mrs Lively crossly. 'So stop messing around. I'll count to ten, Luke. If you haven't told me the truth by then, I'll . . .'

'Turn him into a worm.'

Luke felt Gretl's bony grip on his shoulder.

'Just joking!' said Gretl, stepping forward and shaking Mrs Lively's hand. 'I'm Aurora's godmother and you must be Luke's mum. I hope you don't mind me dropping in like this. You must be wondering why Aurora's a bit unusual.'

'I'm not,' squealed Aurora.

'I had been wondering,' said Mrs Lively.

'It's like this . . .' said Gretl, lowering her voice and placing a hand confidingly on Mrs Lively's arm. Luke's mum hurried her off into the front room.

'I wonder what Gretl's telling her,' said Luke. He and Aurora were sitting in the kitchen.

'I expect she's making up a really tragic story about my parents swanning off abroad and leaving me to be brought up by a mad governess.'

'And Mum will fall for it,' said Luke.

'You can't blame her for not believing our story, can you? I'm having the most awful trouble believing it myself.'

'What exactly did happen?' asked Luke. 'Did you prick your finger on a spinning wheel, like it says in the story?'

'No,' Aurora said in a pitying tone. 'Of course not. It was a sewing machine, silly. I was taking it apart to see how it worked.'

Aurora was just about to give Luke a detailed account when Mrs Lively and Gretl came back looking very pleased with themselves.

'Gretl thinks you need to be in full-time education as soon as possible, Aurora, and I agree with her. It's not healthy for a girl of your age to be drifting around in fancy dress.'

'We've been in touch with the Education Department,' said Gretl. 'Once I'd explained things, they said you could go to Luke's school straight away.'

'Luke's school?' said Aurora. 'I don't think I should feel comfortable at a BOYS' school.'

'Mixed,' said Mrs Lively. 'Boys AND girls.'

'Goodness,' said Aurora. 'How modern. But I suppose the girls learn things like sewing and drawing and music, while the boys study science and mathematics?'

'We all get to do everything,' said Luke.

'Unfortunately.'

'Everything!' breathed Aurora. She could hardly believe her luck. 'Even experiments and blowing things up and taking things apart?'

'Er – of course,' said Mrs Lively. 'Otherwise it wouldn't be fair, would it?'

'Mum,' said Luke.

His mum was busy tidying up the spare room so that Aurora could move in.

'What?' said Mrs Lively.

She looked cheerful. There was nothing she liked more than a challenge and Aurora was very challenging indeed. The things that girl said and did! Honestly, if you didn't know better, you'd be forgiven for thinking modern day life had simply passed her by.

'Does Aurora HAVE to go to my school?' said Luke. 'It's not fair. Why can't she go

somewhere else? And why does she have to
come and stay here?'

'I thought you'd like to help her. Poor girl.
Imagine ME going off and leaving you all
alone in the house to get on with things.
Think how YOU'D feel.'

She was tucking in the sheets on the spare
bed, so she couldn't see Luke's face.

'Aurora's godmother is very keen for her to
go to school with you. She told me all about
Aurora's peculiar upbringing. You're the first
real friend she's ever had. Amazing, isn't it?'

Luke's mum shook her head and sighed.
'As for staying here, she can't walk to school,
can she? Not from the castle. It's too far. And
there's no school bus and they can't drive. So,
. unless you've got a better idea . . .'

He hadn't. Worse luck.

Luke tried to argue, but it was no use. 'But
she won't know anything. And she's so old-
fashioned. Everyone'll pick on her and then
they'll pick on me too. It will be terrible.'

'Once she's in school uniform she'll look
just like everyone else. You'll see.'

7

The favour

'There's no way I'm walking in with you
looking like that. Everyone will laugh,' said
Luke, hovering outside the classroom door.
Of the 260 girls at Luke's school, only Aurora
was wearing a long black skirt, lace gloves
and a straw hat as part of the uniform.

'They won't dare,' said Aurora. She
sounded very confident and there was a

determined glint in her eye. She grasped the door handle firmly and swept into the classroom, with Luke trailing behind. There were a couple of giggles and someone sniggered.

They soon stopped when Miss Warbuoys, Luke's terrifying teacher, found herself starting to curtsey. How extraordinary, she thought, as she felt her knees bend and her head dip. Aurora smiled graciously and introduced herself. 'I will sit here,' she said, taking Miss Warbuoy's chair and pulling it up to Miss Warbuoy's desk.

Luke let out a strangled gasp. You could have heard a pip squeak, as the class looked first at Aurora and then at their teacher.

'You have to admit,' said Luke's friend
Winston, as they queued up for lunch, 'it was
a dead impressive thing to do. And old
Warbuoys just let her do it!'

'My mum says she has natural authority,'
said Luke.

They turned to look at Aurora, who was
surrounded by an admiring gaggle of girls.

'Mum got her a uniform, you know, but she wouldn't even try it on. She said there just wasn't enough of it and she'd feel undressed!'

'Not enough uniform. That's weird,' said Winston. 'Most of the girls here think there's way too much.'

They sat in silence for a minute. Then Luke said, 'She's used to wearing layers of clothes. Supposing someone tried to make you go into class just wearing pants.'

'I'd like to see them try,' said Winston.

'So would I,' said Luke.

'Good grief,' said Mrs Lively as they were having their tea after school. 'Did you really sit at Miss Warbuoy's dcsk, Aurora?'

'It was the only one free,' she said absently. She was glued to the T.V. She had the remote control in her hand and she kept flicking channels and turning the sound up and down.

'Don't do that, Aurora,' said Mrs Lively, 'or you'll break it.'

Aurora said, 'Oh, sorry.' But then she discovered the teletext button.

'This is so wonderful. You have no idea!'

'That's nothing to what she did at school, Mum,' said Luke. 'On the Internet. She was through to Number Ten in no time. And she asked to speak to the Prime Minister, saying he was a personal friend of her father's.'

'Is he?' said Mrs Lively in surprise.

At school, Aurora was making quite a reputation for herself. It was a long time since the teachers had taught anyone who was so keen to learn. She wanted to know how *everything* worked. And if no one could explain, she would take things to pieces and find out for herself. Aurora was a hit with the girls too. They'd even started dressing like her.

'Amazing,' said Ron.

The Minister nodded in admiration.

'Things have turned out much better than we could have hoped. Not the traditional ending we've been used to, of course, but perfectly acceptable in this day and age.'

'And more interesting,' said Ron. 'I can't wait to find out what happens next.'

'More interesting, perhaps,' said Gretl, who was back at H.Q. 'But there's still some loose ends that need to be sorted out.'

'What sort of loose ends?' asked the Minister.

'I know that Mama and Papa were in the South of France and Williams and Miss Wibberley ran off before the Big Sleep,' said Gretl, 'but two hundred castle servants have just woken up to find they're a hundred years out of date. Have you thought what's going to happen to them?'

'Er,' said the Minister, looking uncomfortable. 'It's never been a problem before.'

'Two hundred Victorians. What can they do at the beginning of the Twenty-First Century that will pay their wages *and* stop people asking awkward questions?'

'No idea,' said Ron, cheerfully.

The Minister looked blank.

'You can't think of anything?' said Gretl. 'It's lucky I'm still on the case. Dick Whittington owes me a favour. Let's see what he can do for us.'

'What sort of favour?' asked the Minister suspiciously.

'Who do you think sold him the cat?' said Gretl.

8

Ride on!

A few days later, Luke's mum was reading a
letter from school about a trip to Trentham
Towers, number one theme park and brilliant
day out.

'I'd really love to go,' said Aurora. 'I
haven't been to Trentham Towers for ages.
We spent every Christmas there when I was
little.'

'It's VERY expensive. I don't . . .'

'But Mum,' said Luke, 'we've got to go. It's research. We've got to design a theme park for Information Technology. The best one gets entered for a competition sponsored by Sir Dick Whittington. You know, the pest control billionaire who's got a silver rat on the bonnet of his Rolls Royce. First prize is ten state-of-the-art computers for our school.'

'The school could certainly do with them,' said Mrs Lively. 'And if you're keen to do it – I suppose you'd better go.'

'Does Aurora know that the present Duke has turned Trentham Towers into a theme park?' asked the Minister.

'No,' said Ron.

'Ah,' said the Minister.

Aurora was peering out of the coach window.

'What are those people doing?'

'They're queuing up to pay,' explained
Luke.

'PAY!' screeched Aurora. 'You mean the
Duke makes people pay to get in?'

'Of course he does,' said Luke. 'He needs
the money.'

'What on earth for?'

'To pay people's wages. To make repairs and pay taxes. Just as you need money to keep Cutforth Castle going. Unless you're going to sell it of course.'

'SELL CUTFORTH CASTLE?' said Aurora. 'Of course I'm not. What a stupid idea.'

'I hope you've got lots of cash then,' said Luke.

'I certainly have,' said Aurora, wondering what cash was and where she could get some.

'Has she?' Ron asked the Minister.

'Unfortunately not,' he replied. 'Prince Hugo was the one with all the money.'

Ron let out a long, low whistle. 'Shivering whippets!'

'Why is that woman wearing such silly clothes?' Aurora demanded as a Queen

Elizabeth the First look-alike strolled past.

'Trentham Towers is a theme park,' explained Luke patiently. 'It's supposed to be set in Elizabethan times.'

'People pay to see this sort of thing, do they?'

'Yes, but there are rides as well. Most people come to go on those.'

'Rides?' asked Aurora. 'What sort of rides?'

9

Wait and see

Aurora was watching the corkscrewing
Dangle of Death with absolute concentration.
Then she said, 'But how will I keep my hat
on when we're hanging upside down?'

'I'll hold it for you while you go on,' said
Luke.

'Don't be silly,' she said, marching him
straight to the head of the queue. (No one

complained. They thought she was part of the show.) 'You're coming with me. We have to experience *everything*, or we won't be able to design our own park.'

'We?' said Luke. 'Who said that I was going to be your project partner?'

'It's up to you,' she said, fastening herself firmly into one of the ride's bucket seats. 'But I've got a really good idea that will win us that prize. An idea that will mean I'll never have to sell Cutforth and move away.'

Luke opened his mouth to say 'I wouldn't mind if you did move', but the words didn't seem to want to come out. Just think: no more waiting hours to use the bathroom. No more having to share his computer. No more embarrassment as Aurora showed him up in public by getting all excited about escalators, supermarkets, skateboards and telephone kiosks. Still, he thought he might even miss her. Life hadn't been quite so dull since she'd moved in.

'All right then,' he said, grudgingly. 'But

don't blame me if whizzing upside down at sixty miles an hour makes me sick.'

*   *   *

By the time they got home, Luke was worn out. Aurora had made him try each ride at least twice and they'd sat through three different shows.

'Raiders of the Lost Potatoes was awesome,' said Aurora. She was standing in the kitchen eating a packet of cheese and onion crisps.

'The bit where Sir Walter Raleigh stole the potatoes from under the noses of those pirates was dead impressive. Who'd have thought potatoes could be so exciting?' said Luke.

Aurora nodded. 'We can have the same sort of thing in *Victorian World*, only not with potatoes.'

'*Victorian World?*'

'Our theme park,' said Aurora.

'No way,' said Luke. 'We'd never win the prize with an idea as boring as that.'

'It won't be dull at all,' said Aurora crossly.
'Why does everyone think the Victorians are
boring? Look at all the exploring and
inventing we did. Wait and see. It won't be
boring at all.'

Luke had been waiting for days, but Aurora wouldn't show him what she was doing.

'It's my project as well,' he shouted. He was just about to start banging on the spare room door, when she came out looking pleased with herself.

'There,' she said, handing Luke a beautiful hand-coloured sketch of *Victorian World*.

'It's brilliant. Very artistic,' said Luke.

'Look,' she said. 'Here is Cutforth right in the middle. I thought we'd open it to the public. We won't even have to get the staff to pretend to be Victorian! Outside we'll have the Victoria Falls flume. That will be part of Dr Livingstone's African Adventure. Then I thought we'd have Stephenson's Wild Ride, Dickens' World, Edison's Electric Emporium, Grimaldi's Big Top . . .'

'But . . .'

'But?'

'This will look great on the front of the *Victorian World* programme, but inside we need a proper plan, with each ride drawn

accurately. Come and look at my theme park
game on the computer. Once we've had a
good look at the castle, we can customize it
and print out a proper programme. Your
drawing on the front. My plan inside.'

'*Our* plan,' said Aurora firmly. 'I shall be asking the Head Gardener for his detailed map of the castle grounds. He's measured every inch of the estate already.'

'Terrific,' said Luke. 'That will save a mountain of work. But there's still loads to be done and only a few weeks to do it.'

10

Winner takes all

'That's it,' said Aurora, as they handed in
their theme park competition entry. 'We've
done the best we can.'

'You certainly have,' said Mrs Lively.

She was impressed. She had never seen
Luke work so hard on anything before. The
last two weeks had been blissful. He hadn't
moaned about being bored once.

She was a bit worried about her phone bill
though. They seemed to have spent a lot of
time making long-distance calls and sending
faxes to firms with names like Batty's
Engineering, Theme Dream and Rides R Us.

But it had paid off. When they showed her the finished project, she was amazed at all the detail they had put into it.

'How on earth did you manage it?' she gasped. 'You've even found out how much it would cost!' She thought the only thing Luke knew about money was how to spend it.

'Oh, that was easy,' said Aurora. 'It's amazing what information people will give away. That nice woman at Trentham Towers was really helpful.'

'I think you deserve to win. I really do,' said Mrs Lively, giving them both a big kiss. 'If that Sir Richard's got any sense, he'll think so too.'

'Of course he will,' said the Minister. 'Won't he?'

'Probably,' said Gretl. 'He's a very clever business man. As soon as I mentioned Cutforth Castle, he could see the possibilities.

I could almost see the pound signs flashing in front of his eyes.'

'Then he'll give them the prize. Besides, I thought he owed you a favour.'

'He did. But he paid that back by setting up the competition. He made me agree that Aurora and Luke would only win if they deserved to. He said he has his reputation to think of.

First time for everything, I suppose. Anyway,'
she said slyly, 'I think you'll find that they do
win. She's a clever young lady and Luke isn't
quite the dead loss I thought he was going to
be. They work well together. I just had to
nudge things along in the right direction.
Didn't take much. A phone call here, a word
there. Nothing any other godmother
wouldn't do.'

Meanwhile, at the Albert Hall, where the
Awards Ceremony was about to take place, Sir
Richard was feeling jittery. He'd been feeling
jittery ever since Gretl had started him on the
idea of theme parks. He knew this was his
chance to make a fortune. But would Gretl
tell everyone he was trying to make money
out of school children? Had she seen through
him? He came out in a cold sweat every time
the competition was mentioned. This was
quite often, because the Press had heard

rumours that he was planning to branch out of pest control and into leisure management.

'Was Sir Richard hoping to use the winning competition entry as a blueprint for a new theme park?' they kept asking. 'And if so, did he have a site in mind?'

At last he saw the winning entry. He'd been careful not to judge the competition himself. He had a whole committee to blame if things went wrong. Still, as it happened, he didn't have to worry. He rubbed his hands together in glee.

Luke and Aurora's entry had been magnificently thought out. It was a clear winner – and now he could think about making it a reality.

'Cutforth Castle,' sighed Sir Richard happily. 'What a dream of a place! It's miles from anywhere, but close to everything!'

All he had to do now, was to talk terms with the castle's owner. She was only a young slip of a girl, so there couldn't be any problems. His lawyers would have the contract drawn up and signed in no time.

He stepped forward towards the microphone, with a big white envelope in one hand.

'I won't feel happy until we know who's won,' said the Minister, who was watching the Awards Ceremony live on Fickle's monitor.

Gretl didn't say anything, but she wouldn't feel happy either.

'And the winner is . . . Aurora Rams-Botham
and Luke Lively of Osgathorpe Upper School.
Give them a big round of applause, ladies
and gentlemen.'

Aurora and Luke were quickly propelled on
stage.

'And . . .' Sir Richard held up his hand for
silence, 'I'd like to make another
announcement. As long as Miss Rams-
Botham and I can do a deal . . . and I'm sure
we can . . . I'm planning to open a real
Victorian World at Cutforth Castle, this time
next year.'

'That's BRILLIANT!' whispered Luke to Aurora, who was standing right next to him.

'Imagine! All our rides in action. We never thought you'd be able to afford to do that.'

But strangely enough, Aurora did not look pleased. She was about to speak, when something totally unexpected happened.

'Good grief!' gasped the Minister. 'What on earth is HE doing here?'

'Who?' asked Ron, peering hard at Fickle's monitor.

'Don't you recognize him? It's Prince Hugo! I thought he'd run off with his Personal Fitness Trainer.'

'He did,' said Ron. 'But his father cut him off without a penny, so he dropped Paula like a hot potato.'

'Serves him right,' said the Minister.

'I hope he isn't going to mess things up,' said Gretl.

'What do you mean?' asked the Minister, sounding alarmed.

'Prince Hugo is very good looking,' said Gretl.

'But he's not very nice,' said Ron indignantly. 'She wouldn't choose him instead of Luke, would she?'

'We'll have to wait and see,' said Gretl. 'Won't we?'

By this time, dark and handsome Prince Hugo was on stage and down on one knee in front of Aurora.

'Ooh,' gasped the audience. Things were looking up.

'Cast aside this spotty, puny apology for a prince,' breathed Prince Hugo, sneering at Luke. 'Let me whisk you away to a new life.'

'Aah,' sighed the audience. This was more like it.

'Certainly not,' said Aurora.

'But I'm Hugo. Don't you know who I am?'

Aurora looked cross. She did know who he was. He was the dark and handsome prince of her dreams. The one who should have woken her up with a kiss.

As it was, Luke had done it instead. She glanced across at him. He was jiggling up and down on the spot, looking even more uncomfortable than normal. He was really quite endearing.

'I don't want a new life,' she said, scowling at Hugo. 'Now that I'm into it, I'm really enjoying this one. I bet the only reason you're here is because you think I'm going to sell Cutforth Castle to Sir Richard for millions of pounds.'

Sir Richard beamed and nodded approvingly.

'But I'm not.'

Sir Richard stopped beaming.

'At least Luke's not after my money. So you can clear off, Hugo, because I don't need you.'

'Oh, I say,' said Prince Hugo. 'But we're supposed to live happily ever after. It says so in all the books.'

'This is the Twenty-First Century for goodness sake,' said Aurora. 'I don't need to choose a husband from a book.

'And by the way,' she said, turning to Sir Richard, 'if you still want to talk about *Victorian World*, send me a fax tomorrow. At Luke's house.'

'Oh,' said Luke, still jiggling a bit, 'you're still staying with us then?'

'Of course,' said Aurora. 'As long as you don't mind.'

'Suppose not,' said Luke, trying to sound casual.

'I'm going to need a lot of help,' she said.

'What with?' asked Luke.

'*Victorian World*. I'm not going to let Sir Richard take the whole thing over. It will have to be a three-way partnership. That way we'll always be able to out-vote him.'

'Three ways?' asked Luke.

'Me, you and Sir Richard of course. You ARE going to be my partner, aren't you?'

'Of course!' said Luke. 'Does that mean I'll get paid?'

'Maybe,' said Aurora. 'But only if you help me with something else as well.'

'What?' asked Luke, suddenly suspicious.

'History homework,' said Aurora looking very serious. 'I'm very good up until 1895. After that it's more or less a complete blank. Have I missed much?'

'Two world wars,' said Luke airily, 'women getting the vote, manned space flight… And that's just for starters.'

'Jolly good,' said the Minister as they watched Luke and Aurora wander off in search of Mrs Lively. She'd heard that Sir Richard was looking for a new accountant, so she was lying in wait for him, off-stage. 'A happy ending after all. We won't have to worry about the next Sleeping Beauty for ages, either.'

'No,' said Gretl. 'Thank goodness. But I've still got the Three Pigs to sort out.'

'Really?' said the Minister. 'I thought they were pretty straightforward.'

'They were,' sighed Gretl, 'but these days people *want* to make houses out of wood and straw. It's a very ecological thing to do. So I think the tale needs a little tweak for the Twenty-First Century.'

'Radical,' said Ron.

About the author

Fairy stories have fascinated me since I was knee high to a wicked witch. Some of them made me anxious: *Snow White, The Snow Queen, Hansel and Gretl*. Some of them made me smile and cheer: *Three Billy Goats Gruff, Three Little Pigs, Jack and the Beanstalk*.

All of them made me think and one of them, *Sleeping Beauty*, made me think so hard, I decided to write my own version of it!

You see, there was one thing about the story I could *never* understand:

Everyone in the castle goes to sleep for a hundred years and when they wake up, nothing's changed.

Really! I mean, how likely is *that*?